Young Learner's

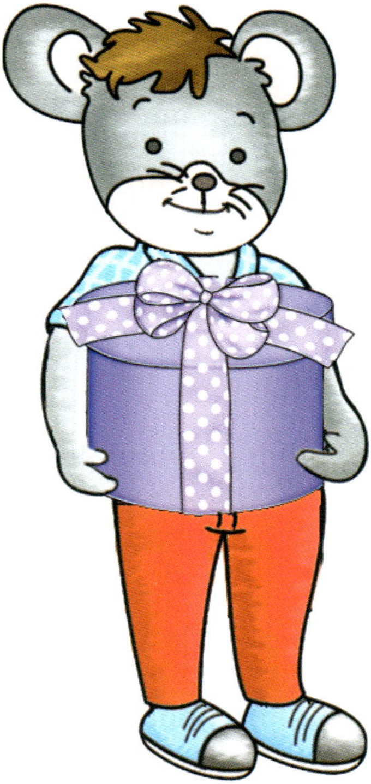

Nibs Makes Amends

Sangita Koushik

Nibs lived with his parents and younger sister, Dibs. Nibs and Dibs were very fond of each other.

They shared their toys, and loved playing with each other. Their favourite playing spot was the beach.

One day, they were playing in their playroom. They started fighting over a small matter.

Nibs got so angry with Dibs that he broke her favourite doll. Little Dibs started crying.

Nibs left her crying and went to his own room. By evening, Nibs had forgotten all about the fight with Dibs. He was all dressed up and ready to play.

He went looking for Dibs as it was time to play on the beach. She was sleeping in her room. The broken doll was lying by her side.

Now, Nibs felt very bad. He had broken her doll in anger, but he loved his sister.

He realised that he had hurt Dibs a lot. He knew that it was her favourite doll.

Nibs decided to make up for his wrong actions. He went running to his room. He took out his money box.

He broke it open. He put all the money in his pocket and went to a big toy shop near their house.

He looked for the best doll in the shop.
He found one and bought it.

He got it packed in a nice purple box.
Then, he rushed home.

At home, he found Dibs sitting with the broken doll. He said, "I am sorry for what I did. See, I have got something for you." Nibs gave her the gift box.

Dibs was surprised. She quickly opened the box. Her face lit up when she saw the doll. It was the prettiest doll she had ever seen!

She kissed her brother happily and said, "Nibs, this doll is very pretty. Thank you so much!" Nibs was happy too for having made amends.

Moral: Always admit your mistakes and make amends for them.

Printed in India